Wild Talk

Jane Martin

SAMUEL FRENCH

FOUNDED 1830

SAMUELFRENCH.COM
SAMUELFRENCH-LONDON.CO.UK

FOR PRODUCTION ENQUIRIES

UNITED STATES AND CANADA
Info@SamuelFrench.com
1-866-598-8449

UNITED KINGDOM AND EUROPE
Plays@SamuelFrench-London.co.uk
020-7255-4302

Each title is subject to availability from Samuel French, depending upon
country of performance. Please be aware that *WILD TALK* may not be
licensed by Samuel French in your territory. Professional and amateur
producers should contact the nearest Samuel French office or licensing
partner to verify availability.

MUSIC USE NOTE

Licensees are solely responsible for obtaining formal written permission from copyright owners to use copyrighted music in the performance of this play and are strongly cautioned to do so. If no such permission is obtained by the licensee, then the licensee must use only original music that the licensee owns and controls. Licensees are solely responsible and liable for all music clearances and shall indemnify the copyright owners of the play(s) and their licensing agent, Samuel French, against any costs, expenses, losses and liabilities arising from the use of music by licensees. Please contact the appropriate music licensing authority in your territory for the rights to any incidental music.

IMPORTANT BILLING AND CREDIT REQUIREMENTS

If you have obtained performance rights to this title, please refer to your licensing agreement for important billing and credit requirements.

WILD TALK was first produced at the Greer Garson Theatre on October 16, 2015 in Santa Fe, New Mexico. The performance was directed by Jon Jory, with sets by Laura Fine Hawkes, costumes by Marcia Jory, props by Jocelyn Manning, and sound by Emily Curley. The Production Stage Manager was Reagan Roby. The cast was as follows:

STRIKE UP	Joey Beth Gilbert
CHOPIN	Tristine Henderson
ORDINARY	Sarah Spickard
JANET DE MOULIAN	Madeleine Garcia
JAKE	Rachel Wagner
SHASTA RUE	Alexis Lacey
FORD PICK UP	Megan Kelly
FOOTBALL	Laila Mae James
PAJAMAS	Donna Bella Litton
THE END	Lauren Trujillo

STRIKE UP

(A marching band crescendo. Lights up. A drum majorette. She raises her hand. Silence.)

CHARITY. Musicians at rest!

(Looks us over.)

My name is Charity "Hot Damn" Godswill and I am the best drum majorette in the world, hands down. Y'all have come to see the parade today but my little darlin's we have bigger fish to fry.

(Sees something.)

Hoss, you better move that Thunderbird off the route. You got no idea what's coming down. I have led maybe a thousand parades in my time, but this one takes twenty-seven hours to pass any given point, and you don't want those footprints all over your car.

(To someone in the crowd.)

Shut that pretty little baby up now. Kootchie, kootchie coo.

(Back to her story.)

I was lead majorette at Bama' where I averaged fourteen marriage proposals after every game plus enthusiastic invitations to the Kama Sutra. Citizens, before the last glockenspiel passes your blanket, your life, gauran-damn-teed, will be changed for ever. Now, breathe, through your nose and follow me close. Man is the scariest, most violent and dangerous pack animal in the universe. The only place you can love man in a pack is in a parade. Period. That subject is closed.

(Blows the whistle around her neck.)

I was a troubled child. I bit my mother's nipples off and just took it from there.

(Tosses peppermints into the crowd.)

Y'all suck on those. I used to hate everybody. I was a spitter. Never missed a tuba as it went by. No dude would come near me. At least not in good clothes. I was so bad that from sheer nasty I wore myself down to eighty seven pounds and had shingles all over my body. Hoss, you put that nasty girl down you never know where she's been. My dada drug me all over the continent to get my mind straight, Adlerian therapy, Freudian therapy, Jungian Therapy, Behavioral Modification, Coherence Therapy, Holotropic Breathwork, eye movement desensitization. Hell I spit on more therapists then you could count. My mood was so black you could shine it at a shoeshine stand. Finally got me some nylon paracord, fashioned me a hangman's noose, got up on a rickety chair, and then just in time, just barely, far off, I heard a marching band strike up "American Patrol."

(We hear it too.)

And lost in the Devil's despair, my foot started tapping, I started to whistle, my eyes dilated and I lept from a third-floor window, killing a coyote, breaking my arm, and with the bone exposed, staggered to my feet, covered in blood, one finger snapped off, I called cadence and quick stepped out in front of that band. And I say to the multitudes, I never looked back because I realized I could love mankind in a parade! I could love 'em to the east, I could love 'em to the west, I could love 'em in the wild ass dunes of the Gobi Desert riding a two-humped Dromedarius through a plague of locusts. And so my chicks, my chucks, my raggedy ass humanity, we've got a life's work dead ahead of us so strike up!

(The band plays "Seven Nations Army.")

Babies, you will see you today what you have never seen, hear what you have never heard and have your fill of peppermints. We are coming by you a two hundred thousand strong international, interracial, intergenerational marching band of every sexual orientation! I got a grant. Horn section of one hundred thousand, forty-thousand drummers, a slew of them one-handed, ten thousand tubas to spit in, ten thousand gay flautists, fifteen thousand Cowboys on Palomino horses, five thousand clowns in little red cars, nine thousand beauty queens, two of them brunette, thirteen tap dancing bears, and the presidents of one hundred and forty countries dressed as orchids and singing *kumbaya*. We are stepping out from LA to New York, Costa Rica, the shores of Tripoli, seven continents Iceland, and Waco Texas. And everywhere we go the crowds are dressed as Disney princesses, the Chippendales, zombies, and the winners of Cosplay, fall in behind playing finger whistles 'til there is nobody left for the wars and there will be, mark my words, Peace on Earth and peppermints for everybody!

(The band segues into "Thunder and Blazes.")

Y'all better get on home now and get your costumes on, bring a few sandwiches but we have corndogs for everybody. Pull your trombones out of the closet. Gentleman dust off your piccolos.

(pause)

Big mama get that Bichon Frisé out of the street. One natural minute till we step off with me high kicking out front and change in the world.

(Blows her whistle.)

Flag girls hold steady! Drum Corps on the count of eight! Toss those dancing bears the steaks! Crowd start Tapping your feet. Open your eyes and your icy hearts. Showtime! Let's move it out! Yes, oh yes, it is the rapture burst out of the clouds. It's the rapture washing our hearts of sin and committing our feet to the dust of the road! Rock it out! Quickstep! Blow Gabriel.

("Saints Go Marching In.")

Saints go marching in. Have y'all a peppermint! Damn I'm happy! Roll Tide

(Blackout.)

CHOPIN

(A middle-aged woman, perhaps a teacher, very carefully dressed sits in a vintage armchair. A chair across from her remains empty. Chopin is playing.)

BETTY. *Andante Spianato et Grande Polonaise brillante.* Opus 22. I think. Chopin, of course. A day with fourth graders requires Chopin, don't you think? He was Polish, of course, as was my father. Baczchochwski. I just tell fourth graders the Chowski part. Then, as you know, Chopin moved to France, and my mother, Adele the ferocious, was French. When she understood they would cease production of nylons during the war, she emptied her account and bought a hundred pairs, which lasted her until she was eighty-three and then died. On purpose.

(Points to herself.)

Betty Baczchochwski. "Betty", which I don't much care for. My friend Lois who is my principal calls me "Double B." If I itemize, she is my only amusing friend.

(She gestures to the empty chair.)

Do you see? In the chair? Of course you don't. It was a pretension to ask.

(She smiles at the chair.)

My memory is that I noticed him when I was three or four. Mother didn't see him of course, and my father sometimes pretended on and off, but I have always. He's wearing what I think in the forties they called an "Esquire Jacket", navy of course, double breasted. And the hat. He never takes off the hat. He's my death sitting in a chair. At school he leans against the door. In the car, he rides in the back seat. In the grocery store he prefers the cereal aisle. Death, to be clear is always where I am. You have one too. But he tells me they are never visible. He tells me that I am the only person he knows of that sees their death. A design flaw, I should think. Because I see him, have always seen him, he will speak to me occasionally, but I would have to call him taciturn. The story seems to be that when we pass... die...we all become someone else's death for a lifetime. No one you know, which I think is quite empathetic. I gather it's a form of on the job training or...well, really, I'm not sure. I have never been vouchsafed the organizing principle, he never speaks of that. He will however, once in a blue moon, talk about his job when Chopin is playing. No other composer seems to provoke or allow it.

Do you think me quite mad? Perhaps I am, but in the main I am perceived, or rather dismissed as all too sane. People at parties tend to wander off because my rationality bores them. Well, I can satisfy you on certain points.

(Music changes.)

Nocturne in F Major. Your death is empowered to choose the moment of your decease and its manner. For them it's a kind of essay question. It could be, for instance, to prevent something you might do or experience. It could be illustrative for others. Or, perhaps, impulsively, because your death simply chose to do it. In the larger picture that also has meaning, but he does not or cannot divulge that. He did, given my awareness of him, and having gotten into the sherry, tell me about his departure. It was after the prom, which made the day special. He and a girl he only identified as "kitten" waltzed off something called the Cowen Park Airborne Bridge, quite unintentionally and fell to their, well, deaths. They had apparently never kissed. Who knows why his death chose that. He told me he has to point at you. Mother taught me, of course, that pointing was rude because such an indicative gesture assigns blame. Apt, don't you think? The pointing stops your breath. This does not, for instance, prevent, or for that matter encourage suicide. Let us say they had chosen to leap from the Cowen Park Bridge. If your death points at you, you die, otherwise you bob back to the surface quite alive. The impulse is yours, the result, Deaths. "On to the point", as mother would say. Well, the point for me, seeing him as I do, is not the frightening, even tragic, aspect but rather makes life more thrilling, much as Chopin does.

(She looks at the chair.)

I think I've come to have a little crush on him. So dapper, the little pencil moustache, the shoes so highly shined. I've come to find it quite endearing.

(She blows him a kiss and then looks back to the audience.)

If your death is at arms length you become more present, more acute, more alive even, perhaps, a better teacher, and your pulse, your heartbeat, your breath are little miracles…infinitely rare. At first I hated seeing him, but now with Chopin playing, and the snow… I am so sorry that you can't see yours. It does make it necessary to consider a time when I will be someone else's death. To sit in a chair next to you wearing…what will I be wearing? Something welcoming. Something blue. Present at the panoply of your life, and then, the moment I imagine endlessly, the moment I will only understand at that moment when I…

(Raising her arm and pointing out into the audience.)

Do this.

(Chopin plays on.)

(Blackout.)

ORDINARY

WOMAN. These colors don't match, huh? I don't have good
taste, I don't. But everybody longs for beauty, huh.
Can't dress me up though, ordinary is just how I look.
Hardly have a distinguishing feature, darn it. You know
what I'm talking about. I don't have to break it down,
huh? Lots of people are scared of the ordinary like it
was a vampire. They just run from it. Wrinkled old guys
driving red convertibles, waitresses at Denny's telling
people they're witches. Scrawny busboys getting all
tattooed up. Stuff like that. I could just never get my
underwear in a twist over it. I was really at home in the
ordinary. Sat comfortable in it like an old chair. I don't
know about you but I never cared to be singled out,
didn't care to be looked at, kind of a natural background
kind of individual. Just lived in the ordinary real relaxed
like they tell me a person feels after a massage. My
husband Juergan he liked I was a gray person because
he admired to shine. Shoot, I liked to see him do it.
He just runs the body shop down at the garage but he
can juggle oranges, chainsaws, tiki torches. We had the
marriage thing down because we balanced out. That
was right up to the birthday party. We got a two year
old, Juergan named Minerva. Last Wednesday was her
birthday party we did it up, streamers and balloons in
the yard. There were six or seven neighbors and it went
real well. After everybody ate casserole and went home,
I just left the mess out in the yard 'til Juergan came
back from bowling league. Put Minerva down and
watched my show. I guess Juergan went out for beers,
so I trucked on out to clean up. We had those floaty
balloons. I forget what you call the stuff you blow them
up with. I want to say hydrogen peroxide, but that's
not right. Anyway this one balloon had got loose, but
it had lost its oomph and it was kind of floating there
about six inches above where I could reach. So you
know, I just tried a little jump, which I'm not real good

at, carrying the weight I do. Just bent my knees a little
for the spring-off, jumped up to get that peach colored
balloon and I went up about eight feet judging by our
six foot fence and then I came down easy like goose
down, sweet and slow, didn't hurt myself at all. And
I just stood there, arms at my side under that velvet sky,
big dipper hanging down in the back yard, in amongst
the dirty paper plates and scrunched up wrapping
paper, knowing what was couldn't be. I wasn't high.
Hadn't smoked a bowl or anything like that. Didn't
have a screw loose so far as I could tell. After a little bit,
my mind quieted down and my hands quit shaking, so
I coiled up and tried it again and up I went, easy as easy,
up past the tip of the pear tree. And I pushed down on
the air like this, and I kept on doing that 'til I was free
and clear and then I just swam the breast stroke, and
there was just nothing you could call it, but I could fly.
I could. And I swear on the bleeding heart of Jesus and
Minerva's blue eyes that's what I did. Up past where the
hawks circle in summer.

    (Long pause.)

I didn't tell Juergan because he'd right away see the
money in it. He'd have me flying into the Super Bowl
at half-time, stuff like that. And all that attention,
all that hubbub would be an agitation and a foreign
country to me. 'Cause I got my life in the ordinary.
Didn't feel like I could handle that 'cause being looked
at always cut me like a knife. I tried, but, I couldn't stop
for a while because it was so beautiful and I got to know
what that was. Sometimes I thought I might just fly 'til
I fell from the sky from starvation. That, and I knew
I'd get found out some way, get seen by one of those
traffic helicopters or something like that and I would
never get back to my ordinary ever and I'd get myself
seen. And I told myself you have to stay with what you
are. But, one night when I came back in the window
I was thinking how it's not going to work out to be what
you're not no matter how pretty and high it might be

and there was Juergan's juggling stuff left out on the sofa and I just stood there taking that in, thinking about his shine. Then I went up to bed and lay down with Juergan snoring beside me and the moonlight coming in big through the window. And I pushed down a little, went up about a foot, and it came to me, if I can do this, that must be who I am. And I just floated there a couple minutes and then I reached down and shook his shoulder and I said, "Wake up Juergan, I can fly."

(Blackout.)

JANET DE MOULIAN

(A young woman trips on in full Pierrette white. She has a small red basket full of rose petals and helium and balloons on a string. She's accompanied by merry twinkling clown music. Centerstage she delicately releases the balloon, which was out of sight. She waves to it.)

JANET. *Adieu ma belle amie.*

(She moves downstage tossing a handful of red petals into the audience.)

I am Janet De Moulian and I am unbearably happy. Really, I would do anything to be released from the prison of my delight. My body reeks of joy when I see a sunset, a mountain, a child, a chair, a bottle of balsamic vinegar. I explode with love and wild delight when I see my mother, my brother, my boyfriend, my dentist, a corpse.

(She laughs merrily.)

Yes, I laugh. I'm laughing all the time. I don't get any sleep because I wake up hilarious every half hour. Why am I laughing? I have no idea. Yesterday, driven by madcap fancy I found myself in a Halloween boutique and bought...

(She gestures at her costume.)

This ridiculous outfit and I haven't taken it off, I showered in it, I slept in it. Yesterday I was laughing at cockroaches, giggling and recycling containers. I'm ecstatic when I clean out the cat litter. Euphoric at disposing of maxi pads, delighted when I broke out in hives... What's happening to me?!

I think this all started last Wednesday when there were thousands of flying ants on my apartment wall. I got switched to the night shift. I dropped my cell phone in a milkshake and I said to myself, Janet, I said, you cannot control events but you can control how you react to event and that triggered the Charles dickens quote: "You wear the chains you forged in life." And that's true, it's so true, and at that moment my chains fell away and I was magically free of moods, the unhappiness, the anger that have plagued me all of my life. Why be revolted by cockroaches, they're little Pierrots enjoying them. But what was unexpected was that the Charles Dickens quote running through my head reconfigured the pathways of my thoughts like a river cutting through farmland and now I'm trapped as one might be trapped in an elevator, walled in by a crippling cascade of positive feelings.

(She begins to tap dance.)

Be still my feet!

(They obey.)

I fell in love six times yesterday. Once with a man and his Shih Tzu, once was a man dressed as the Statue of Liberty, then three identical moving vans. I went to breakfast and the fry cook was like six-four, and three hundred and fifty pounds, tattooed with the entire lyrics of "We are the Champions" with multiple eyelid piercings and giant red, white and blue earplugs and he slapped the eggs down in front of me and yelled, "two eggs murdered with virgin toast!" And I grabbed his arm, kissed him ferociously and in a guttural voice I'd never heard before, I said, "It is imperative that I have your children." He seemed terrified and said, "Let go, lady!" And I said, "I can't, you are my all, my everything, my little pooky-wooky." And I attached myself to him like an octopus. And, he yelled, "Give me a hand here." And two obvious gang members and the lesbian waitress threw me in the street and I screamed, "I love you! I love you tattooed man!" And I was bruised and scratched and humiliated and I was happy. So happy. And I stood in the middle of the intersection transfixed by the delicate beauty of that crosstown bus. I hugged several Japanese tourists and joined a homeless man and his cardboard box. I realized it had always been my dream to live in a box. My destiny.

(She yells, arms extended like wings.)

"I am a prisoner of happiness and it's all Charles Dickens' fault!"

(She speaks immediately to us.)

I would kill, literally kill for a negative feeling or the blessed relief of a little depression. Those among you who long for happiness, who desire above all things, love, delight, pleasure, and appreciation you have no idea that it is all a poisoned well, because the nexus of all pleasure is not pleasure, it is variety. Blessed contrast, the ecstasy of change, the roller coaster ride of highs and lows.

It is too late for me. I'm happy without surcease. People are first attracted and then repulsed. No one can stand that much happiness. It is unutterably vulgar.

(She smiles and then a small giggle escapes her like a bubble. She sings, simply and delightfully.)

PACK UP YOUR TROUBLES IN YOUR OLD BAG AND SMILE, SMILE, SMILE.
WHILE YOU'VE A LUCIFER TO LIGHT YOUR FAG.
SMILE BOYS THAT'S THE STYLE.

(She stands on smiling as the red balloon floats down.)

(Blackout.)

JAKE

WOMAN. Okay, Jake, I have to do this. I haven't been coming out here. I've thought about coming, I think about it every day. I have really but… I'm trying to stop thinking about you Jake and there's not much else to do out here. Seriously Jake, there's not much here that can help either of us. Desiree says a cemetery is memory central…if that's what you're looking for… just the graves and the stones and the trees and the little flags and the plastic flowers and the stuffed animals…and Desiree is right, there are no distractions from the thoughts…the thoughts that are you Jake. I finally came because I have to tell your grave I need to stop thinking of you, Jake. I have to forget that you are the only person that I know for sure loved me. I counted up all the men who said they loved me… I got to seventeen and none of them lasted more than two years, thank God. You hung in there. Whatever love is you took a shot at it every day. And that was incredibly necessary to me Jake. You hardly ever said it, but you absolutely did it every day, on and on. You never took a vacation. I knew I was at the top of your list. You mind if I have a beer? I brought it to help me do this.

> *(Takes a beer out of her shoulder bag. She opens it with a silver church key hung around her neck.)*

Silver church key, birthday present number one. Oh look, there's the older grave digger out stealing flowers. Well, everybody has to make a living.

> *(Takes a swig.)*

Yes, Samuel Adams. "Carbonated piss with molasses added." I remember the quote and the place and the company. I remember way too many things you said. I'm noticeably silent now, people notice that, you spoiled me for conversation mainly. Actually I haven't said this many things in a row since… I can't even understand what I mean when I talk. Its like aphasia.

(Drinks.)

I'm really mad at you Jake for dying. I'm mad at you for not finding out early enough. I'm mad at you for not telling me as soon as you knew. I'm mad at the way the hospital smelled and most of all I'm furious that there is no you to be furious with. It's so unkind Jake because all of this is such an empty gesture which is why I don't come out here. That and the fact that the younger gravedigger hits on me. There must be some girls who like the smell of formaldehyde.

(Kills the bottle.)

It is really tasteless to have to make you up, Jake.

(Puts bottle in her bag.)

The three times I came out here the woman wearing the red hats was always here two graves over. I miss her today because she's big help to the absurdity. Once she played the accordion, it was like being in a demented Paris. Oh, the last time she brought wrapped presents for him. She invited me over to have a piece of cake and wept while we ate. She was really, really nice but she kept pulling her hair while we talked. I kept feeling like I was in a nineteenth century asylum. I still do, Jake, and I'm one of the inmates.

It's such a pain knowing there's no heaven or hell. I kind of liked limbo 'til they got rid of it...limbo had such a hopeful feeling, like knowing a bus would come at 4 pm and get you out of Cleveland. I know I won't be reunited with you. You won't come to meet me in the light-filled tunnel. I know I'll forget what you look like and have to check the photos. I know you don't watch over me and I don't hear the thrumming of your wings. What you are Jake, is irredeemably absent and all the rest is fairy tales. You were my one enormous piece of good luck and when your luck turns, well, it's a very different featureless world and I would get along better in the new world if I wasn't complaining every minute of it to the old one and that feeling is my own personal graveyard where there is no woman in a red hat.

I want revenge. I would like to tear love's little wings off and put its cupid head on a stake by the highway as a warning to others. Some of the best stuff about love is seeing the world through someone else's eyes and now I'm stuck with what I see and I'm just not all that interested in myself and the worst thing is you're still alive in me Jake, taking up all the room and I really need you to be dead. So, I didn't come out here to have a Sam Adams with you, or bring you presents or play the accordion or weep on you I...

(She looks to the left.)

Oh, God, there's the gravedigger.

(Looks back at the grave.)

There's something I have to do, so I won't feel badly all the time, because you are dead Jake but you are believe me, not dead enough. Not dead enough to get me through the day. Just flat out not dead enough.

(She takes a pistol out of her bag. She stares at it.)

You'll get a laugh out of this. I bought it at that gun shop in the Chestnut Tree Mall. The place with all the animal heads in the window and the handmade "Don't Tread on Me" flag. Run by, let us not forget, that creepy guy you went to high school with who served time for skinning cats. He sent you his best.

So, anyway...

(Regards the pistol.)

It's heavy. I like it.

(Looks at the grave.)

Before I came out I burned everything you ever touched, wiped every picture of us off my phone and incinerated the last of your clothes because you are still alive in my heart and that does me great harm. You

would so completely understand this. You would be the
only one who could understand this.

> *(Stares at the gun. Points it and fires five times
> into the grave.)*

Now you're dead.

> *(She walks off.)*

> *(Blackout.)*

SHASTA RUE

(We see a substantial woman and a printed housedress. Over that she wears a beauty contest swag reading "Miss Pretty Belle Kentucky." In her hair is a gold tiara. She carries some slightly wilted yellow roses. She's a plain woman with a mountain of energy that contains elements of the traditional southern tent revival.)

WOMAN. So what you think is wrong with this picture?

(Adjusts her tiara.)

Yeah that's right, Miss Pretty Belle Kentucky. Struck three or four million citizens of the Commonwealth dumb with admiration. Uh huh! The considerable number who is dumb already just got themselves struck dumber. Oh yes, I got the beauty! My big old daughter Shasta Rue, she got it for me. "Don't cry mama." "I ain't crying Shasta Rue." "Cryin' make you wet and ugly." "Ugly already girlfriend, so I'll just get wet." "You cryin' at the TV mama?" "No, I'm just crying for the sheer life of it, honey. Sitting in the trailer, drinking flat falls city beer, lickin' on the taffy Apple, switchin' them channels and just crying all over my miserable low class life." "Hold on there mama." "Say, what? Miss Kentucky pageant on the TV." "Uh Huh." "Looky them beauties, all them anorexic beauties row on row of them." "Reason is ain't enough fat people got a bathing suit." Yes, yes! Me and Shasta looking at them beauties lookin' at all that fine horse flesh. Chilled me to the bone baby, made us mean you know? Gave me and Shasta the bloodlust for straight up bourbon whiskey. Oh fat Jesus, didn't we knock it back? Didn't we drain the cup? Oh yes! Baby Shasta, she got down to panting started in sighin' started in rockin' and rollin' those love handles back to the front the way she does. "How come they don't call out your beauty mama? How come you ain't up there doing the sugar sweet bird calls of the Kentucky Cardinal and your apricot colored one-piece bathin' suit, huh?" "Because, first God made him the pretty. Then he made the plain to make the pretty shine, and then he made us, Shasta Rue, to give them beauties a laugh on Saturday night. Then Shasta commence to bang on the table. She's a big strong girl an' she yells out "An' you made me, didn't you mama? You gave me my poundage an' my six foot one an' my hand can close up over a teapot so y' can't see it, didn't you mama?" "Oh yes, I did that!" An' she yells, "But you left out my glory, left out my beauty, left out my swim suitability," An' I stood up like Moses on the mount an' I point at the TV beauties an' I holler out. "They got it. They got it all." An' she yells, "Let's get it!" An' we do. We haul ass out of that trailer over to Loco boys pick up an' we hotwired that sumbitch and drove eighty-million, lead footed, bumpy-squealin', lay-rubber miles down to Louisville Kentucky, singing "Crazy Train", an' yellin' about them beauties, tears runnin' down our faces, and then we see it. See where they got the pageant. Looming up, all shiny like a jewel box. Searchlights criss-crossin' an' Shasta in the pick up, rockin' doing little whoops. "Whoop! Hit them brakes," she yells. An' I do, I slam em', I bang em' and we go smashin' our heads through that pick up windshield like a kiss through Kleenex, an' were bleeding an' were crying an' we're out of the pick up an' this shrimped up tuxedo doorman says, y'all can't go in there. An' I stomp on his foot and Shasta rips off his lil' blonde toupé an' we wipe off the blood with it an' we're through that lobby eatin' usherettes on the way an' Shasta she hauls open these big old oak doors an' there it is. All gold an' white like heaven itself. We in the theater with the Miss Kentucky Pretty Belle Pageant.

An' there's the beauties, Straight in a line, rainbow dresses an' electric bouquets, smile to smile like one big long picket fence, an' they are waiting on the

envelope for their fate to be delivered by one of them
AC/DC emcees. An' everyone of them ding dong
beauties weighs ninety-seven pounds an' change. An'
Shasta she goes crazy! Sound comes up through her
throat like ash from a volcano an' all the rivers dry
up an' all the dogs an' cats turn to stone an' all over
the town the trees start glowing in the dark an' Shasta
an me start down that aisle, pickin' up speed, rollin'
roarin' and there's ushers steppin' up an' we blow em'
away poppin' up, goin' down, poppin' up, goin' down
an' we speedin', we fly over this pit hole steppin' on
the tubas an' the audience is screamin' an' then, hot
doggies, we up there, we up there with the beauties!
An' Shasta stops, an' the audience it stops, an' the man
with the envelope he stops, an' the big clock on the
balcony it stops, an' it's grave closing, low moanin'
deep down, well water quiet. An' Shasta spreads her
arms, she lets out her wing-span, an' her eyes bug out
an' she says in this deep bass voice, "I come for my
beauty." An' the emcee still smilin', but he got pee pee
seepin' out of the corner of his eye. An' then Shasta,
she throws back her head and crows like a rooster and
we're amongst 'em like a bear is in a rabbit hutch.

Oh there's bouquets flyin' strips of chiffon like a
blizzard, falsies popping out like burger patties, and
store-bought eyelashes rainin' down like a sea of
locusts. Shasta, she stuck two fuck me pumps in the
emcees mouth and kick his Miami tan ass right into
the orchestra pit. I got this one blonde beauty by her
prissy french braids and I'm hootin, "Give me that
uptown wig you baptist bitch." An' then from up on
this high place, clear like a tornado alert comes this
voice singing, "Y'all hold on there Batman and Robin,
back your roly-polies OFF!"

I look up and Shasta she looks up and there she is, slim
as a wand, lightnin' zappin' off her tiara, waist like your
little finger, Miss Kentucky, last year's model, got her
gown on, got her crown on, complexion looking like

she'd been bleached once a day since creation, an' she got crimson red hair like the Devils arsonists just sent her to fire, neon blue eyes flashing on an' off and a little baby sparkles in midst the hairs of her arms an' she says, "What you fat people want?" An' Shasta she shake her hand fist in the air and she stomp on the floor and she says, "I come for my mama's beauty!"

An' Miss Haute Coutre, she walk her pretty perfume tallow-candles self down her red carpet paradise stairs 'til she is nose to nose with Shasta Rue, and she sayin', "Big Honey, you want this raggedy crap, you can sure as hell have it. You can have the crown, the gown, and the chicken à la king. You can pull that parachute off them new Toyotas, dress like Scarlett O'Hairy at the Kosler luncheon an' chap your lips at the kiss-a-queen booth at the hump-a-duck fair." Then she turned to the multitudes an' she says, "You redneck trash, hush up, you hear?" An' she lay her sash on me, gimme her rhinestone scepter, an' slap that gold tiara on my head an' then she smile at Shasta Rue and give her her ear bobs.

And the crowd starts cheering! An' the three of us walk out hand in hand, like a Weight Watchers wet dream of butterball equally. An' the Red Sea parts and we're under the marquee with them searchlights go in an' I say, "Thank you, Miss Skinny." An' she says, "You're entirely welcome, big Mama." An' she unzipped her strapless aquamarine, dot-sequin formal and she say, "They ask you where I gone sweet puffa-billy, you tell them I gone to Houston to dance the foxtrot at the Spoon Gravy Debutante Ball." An' she walks off down main street, naked as a jaybird in her lime green heels, like an exclamation point, whistlin' Dixie. Lemme' tell you one thing, it takes a real lady to walk bare naked through downtown Louisville after 11 o'clock at night and get home safe with two arms and two legs. Yes, oh yesss!

Well, that's how Shasta Rue got me be beauty. Thin
Missy just lay it down like it was spit or ol' gum, but
I know better. Beauty beats smart. Beauty is the life.
Smart just talkin' about it. Uh-huh. See now, I got the
beauty an' you ain't got shit. You want it, you go hunt
some up for your own self. Ain't that right, Shasta Rue?
Pass over that ultra-soft tawny peach, all natural, silky
powder, Revlon blush, baby girl. We on it now!

(Blackout.)

THE FORD PICK-UP

LUCIE. This guy, he took me from my high school when I was fifteen. It was October 27 and the first snow was on the ground. I remember that. He saw me walk out with Ellen McDaniel who was my best friend at that time. He called out my name. He said, "Lucie" and I answered, "Yes, sir." And he said he was Mike somebody or other and that he worked for my dad's construction company in the office and my dad was delayed on the job and he asked Mike to run me home because he knew I had to get ready for the science fair. And that was true, I did. Ellen, she was very careful person and she whispered I oughtn't get into any pick up truck I didn't know for sure and then called out to this Mike, "What's her daddy's first name?" And he smiled a slow smile and said, "Well, his first name is Dawson and his middle name was Victor so if you put it together it was Dawson Victor Delano 5240 West Wilson and he delivered us mechanical drawings at our house several times so maybe he looks familiar?" And I said, "Well maybe." And Ellen look me straight on and said, "Don't you dare Lucie." But I had a lot of lettering left to do on my project which was the effect of an electromagnetic field on single cell organisms which I had to set up in the gym the next morning. So I told Alan she been watching too much television and I hopped in to Mike's ford pick up truck and I didn't see Ellen again for seven years. Mike had a toolshed on his property in Maryland, which is two states over and explained to me that I was his wife now and I will get used to it and like it and when I started screaming he hit me with a wrench and when I woke up I was shackled in the shed. He fed me from McDonald's every single day. I would get the big breakfast with pancakes in the morning and a cheeseburger with fries for dinner, sometimes a milkshake and then when I was finished he would rape me and then play his guitar. I tried yelling and

pounding on the shed when he was gone, but we were
pretty far out, so nothing came of it. I had two babies
which came to be called Mike and Wanda so he had
to move me into the house and he locked us up inside
a room where there is a fridge and baby things. And
Mike would come home at night and it got so I was
glad to see him. And I would ask him what he was
doing and he would describe this job or that job he was
working on. In every couple of years and moved 'til we
ended up outside Toronto Canada and Little Mike he
was ready for preschool and big Mike he came home
one day and said we couldn't go on like we had been
doing because once the kids went to school it would
be all found out, so Mike said we should get all packed
up, and that night we would take a little trip and he
would deliver us back to my daddy, Dawson. And I
cried because I got used to Mike and he was the father
of my children and we got along good now and there
was no force in the arrangment. But Mike said I was a
grown-up woman now and every good thing comes to
an end. But he said he would always stay in touch one
way or the other and he'd be checking on the kids and
I shouldn't cry. And that night he drove us back in the
o0ld white Ford pick up and when the kids were asleep
we stopped at McDonald's for some onion rings and
hamburgers and he explained that love had worked
out every which way in world history, so you couldn't
just say there was a right way to do it. And he said he
would never leave me but then they would lock him up
in prison for the rest of his life and he wasn't made to
stand that and he would think of me every day of his
life and I said I would think of him too and I would
teach little Mike to play the guitar like he did. Then
he apologized for all the distress he had caused me in
those first years, but he could see being twenty years
older than me that my daddy would not have let me
know him. And that is true, my daddy would not. Not
any way in hell. Then we had a real gentle kiss and
Mike he said the truck was running rough and he got

out and opened up the hood, and I disengaged the
break and hit the accelerator and ran him over and
then I backed over him and then I ran over him again
'til he was good and killed. Daddy he was just thrilled
to see me. And the town had a parade for me and the
kids and me can eat free at McDonald's for life. The
kids are doing well. Little Mike has his first science fair
coming up. I keep to myself mainly. I taught little Mike
to play the guitar just like I promised. Sometimes I miss
big Mike pretty fierce. I don't know why I ran over him,
it just came to me in that moment, I don't think I'll
ever love again. I'm still best friends with Ellen. She
says I'm just a one man woman. Maybe that's it. I just
don't know.

(Blackout.)

FOOTBALL

*(A woman is discovered completely togged up for
football helmet, pads, spikes, jersey, the whole deal.)*

WOMAN. Shoot, Louise, I didn't know you were coming
over. Shoot I didn't mean for you to see me like this.

Shoot.

(Takes off helmet.)

Well, Hi! You want some coffee and some spiced apple
cake? Oh well. Louise, I don't know for sure I can
explain this, I really don't. Can I ask you a question,
do you understand men? Well, I know it, I know it,
who does? I mean, God knows I'm trying. Gordie,
he's off for the weekend with guys from work shooting
animals. Now what exactly is the entertainment value
in that? You ever see an animal in his death throes?
Gosh. There was a redheaded finch flew into our big
window yesterday and just lay there on the porch.
I mean I thought the poor thing was deceased, broke
its neck maybe, but when I picked it up in a paper
towel it looked straight at me. Kind of shivering sort of.
I mean I think it was looking for...help...kindness... I
don't know... Looking straight at me like it did, and
then Gordie comes up behind me... Scared the life out
of me... And he said, real brisk "Don't worry honey,
I'll kill it," and he took that little bird in the paper
towel and he went right out on the porch and held
it underwater in the rain bucket and he counted up
to ten seconds like, A thousand one, A thousand two,
A thousand three, and after that he threw it over the
fence. I mean I was kind a like in shock, I guess and
then he came back in and kissed me on the cheek and
he said, "That way, it won't suffer." And then he said,
"How about I fix you a bacon, lettuce, and tomato?",
And off he went. See the thing is, Gordie is the nicest,
tenderest husband in this world, East or West. But he
didn't get it, he didn't get any part of it, he just moved

on like an ocean liner leaving that redheaded finch in its wake. See, what on earth is that? Louise, how on this earth can we understand that? Shoot! What he and his work friends like to do is go out past Waldemere about ten miles where there's this big prairie dog community and sit on these little canvas fold-out stools, and shoot them, a hundred or two. I mean, that's entertainment, Louise. And I sleep with him and I like it! Now, you have walked in on my obsession, which Honey, I never meant for you to know about, or any other human being for that matter. I have to...have to...figure men out, and things aren't looking good. I'm trying to get inside the problem? See? Football. God help us, Football. Gordie drags me over to watch it. He likes a team called L.S.U., which I think is in Los Angeles. Everybody runs different directions and then several three hundred pound men jump on a two hundred pound man and when they get off he staggers up and waves to the crowd and then falls down again and they take him away on a little cart. There's probably a football graveyard somewhere where they put him after they drown him in a rain barrel. I thought maybe if I put on the whole deal like you see here, I would have an insight as to what men like about it. Louise, its real hot and uncomfortable, but I have been going around the house throwing myself into doors, running full steam into the refrigerator. I got me one of those mini watermelon and I carry that around, and I fall on it from time to time. And, I'm here to tell you I did get me an insight. They are sado-masochists, Louise! I am telling you it is clear as day. I asked Gordie would he like to watch the six o'clock news with me on NBC and he said, "No there isn't a good war on." You see how this adds up? Football. They not only want to hurt people, they want to be uncomfortable doing it. Now, women have got them civilized down to a point over thousands of years... I mean, he puts the toilet seat down and they lift up the mattress when you need to clean underneath it. And there is one thing invented which distracts a

males violent tendencies towards himself and others
and that is money. See, money can be pursued, and
must be pursued without empathy, and a profound lack
of empathy explains war, football, and prairie dogs. But
in the pursuit of money, you don't always have to kill
people or knock them down. See, that's progress of a
kind. It allows for there to be birthday parties and what
passes for marriages. But money is worse in the end
because men are not biologically built to share, every
damn one of them wants all the money and boom,
we're right back into the wars. So Louise, I guess what
I think is, we have to get rid of them for the Earth to
survive, and there to be any kind of decent society at
all... For us to be happy, Louise, and every once in
a while go downtown at night. And I was standing in
the living room wondering how football players go to
the bathroom, when it came to me just how that could
work... Just how the earth could survive and how there
could remain a decent caring society on it without
men... I'm just going to say this once, and when you
think it over, you will come to see just how perfect it
is... You ready honey? We got them out numbered so...
Come in a step closer. Now... Poison vaginas.

   (Blackout.)

PAJAMAS

(A young girl, perhaps sixteen, wearing children's pajamas, and terrycloth robe, furry slippers. She carries a well loved teddy bear by one leg. She knocks on our door. We hear the knock. She looks around behind her for a moment. We open the door.)

EMMA. Hi, umm. I'm Emma Elbaz from the little red brick house around the corner on Elm Street. Well, actually it's a little more than a block down. On the left. Well, on the right from here. Or maybe the left. You might remember me from six years of Girl Scout cookies? You were a tagalong. Peanut butter patties. Your neighbor, over there was thin mints. I mean before she died. I was at Sandy's pajama party four doors down. Sandy with the blue hair? That Sandy? I'm having a little crisis of confidence that, ummm, cause a little, well, panic attack at the pajama party and I thought I should seek adult advice because, well really, Sandy's parents don't qualify and my parents...

(Looks at watch.)

Since it's after nine are, ummm, drunk. They are very sweet drunks, this isn't about you know abuse or anything, but their advice after nine is sort of suspect. Please don't phone child services or anything, please? I really love my parents only... I was wondering if you could suggest a future for me? A future? sixteen actually. I know I look younger, but that is possibly because I'm regressing, which is why I brought Nicholas.

(Holds up the stuffed bear.)

Nicholas the bear. Nicholas says hi. I think you are Miss Hendrickson because it says Hendrickson on the mailbox, I'm very glad to meet you and if you could help me out I would be very grateful because, well, after graduation I don't think regression will actually protect me. Do you? I mean given my anxiety disorder? Probably not? Huh? Hmmmmm. Give the onrush of global warming and the uh, rising seas which will put our house underwater, and overpopulation which'll have everybody behaving like rats, and the anti- biotics not working, and the fish all gone and world hunger and continuous wars and not having faith in Volkswagens, I'm just not ready to grow up. See I'm not sure what to count on. My grandfather ran a weekly newspaper and my dad ran that newspaper 'til people stopped reading it, so I guess that's out. And doctor is out because blood makes me puke, and I guess God's on vacation so I can't be a preacher, and I worked as an intern at the car insurance but I kept falling asleep, so I'm having a hard time seeing why regression isn't the best choice. So I'm looking for a little help here because supposedly after high school you can't just stay in your room in pajamas and play Snakes and Ladders. My Aunt Rona married money so that's her suggestion, but as far as I can see, men are just a terrible deal and I don't like the way they smell, which is sort of like they got left out in the rain and their fur got wet. Do I seem negative to you Mrs. Hendrickson, because I don't feel negative. I just mainly feel scared to death.

(Holds up the bear.)

Nicholas is kind of scared too if you take his expression seriously. My mother keeps hiding Nicholas, but I'm afraid she has a rather cruel nature which could possibly come from watching too much television, which if a child like myself took it to be a window on the future you would have to believe vampires are having the most fun. I'm sorry, I don't mean to cry, and this isn't crying, it's just a random tear that broke loose. I know I am taking up your time at a late hour, but I really have a hard time with the panic attacks and I know that somebody nearby, like yourself, an experienced grown-up, has faith in the future that you can...ummm...reassure me, set me on the path

to, well, see, I don't know to what, but I'll bet you
do, right Mrs. Hendrickson? Did I tell you I like your
snowball hydrangeas? The uh, general landscaping is
very encouraging to me. So uh, what is the future for
me? How would you suggest I proceed because as you
can see Nicholas and I are a little stuck.

(Pause.)

Well, I see a tear got loose on you too Mrs.
Hendrickson. I didn't mean to worry you. We will be
all right somehow, right? Oh, I have friends coming
over tomorrow night for monopoly if you would enjoy
that? I can loan you pajamas if you're out? No, that's
fine. We'll thank you very much. Come on Nicholas we
better get home, it looks a little bit like snow.

(Starts off.)

Good night, Mrs. Hendrickson, I am already in the
future from when I started talking to you and see, it's
fine, let's keep that in mind.

(Waves.)

Sing to me Nicholas.

(She exits.)

(blackout)

THE END

(A woman and a power suit. She walks up to lectern. Taps the mike.)

LIZBETH. One, two, three. One, two, three. Good evening. You know me, I am Liz Beth McKay and I have something of crucial importance to say to you. I will not hide my light under a bushel basket. Yes I am wealthy, I am powerful, I am under pressure from the party to run for the Senate. I run marathons, I work selflessly at refugee camps all over the world, and in Louisiana. I date action-movie stars of both sexes, I have two best selling business books, a line of workout gear, I am a co-owner in the NBA, I am currently ranked as the third best vibraphone player in the United States and my saluki key has just won the Westminster dog show.

(She pics the mic from its holder and walks down stage.)

I have two beautiful children, three homes overlooking lakes, degrees from Harvard and the Sorbonne, I have an orchid named after me. I am the subject of a Broadway musical. And, I have been animated by Disney.

(She dabs at her forehead with a scarf and posited into the audience.)

I have cowritten a treaty with the Dalai Llama and my chemists are closing in on a drug that will guarantee me immortality. Your assumption is that my power, my beauty, my wealth, first rate mind, and sense of style guarantee that I am happy, but I am not happy, because I am afraid of trees. They are coming as we speak. You do not have access to the night vision equipment that I do. Delta force does not have access to the night vision equipment that I do. Trees move around at night.

(She suddenly points.)

Don't smirk, you have a red Maple outside your bedroom window? It was there last night, it is there this morning. But is it the same red Maple? No, it is not. My security forces are staking out trees across my estate. Fact.The average red Maple can cover seven miles an hour without attracting attention by moving in bursts. It could be fifty miles away by morning replaced by a second red Maple that looks very much like it.

(She suddenly turns to a different part of the house as if being asked a question.)

Trees do not move when being watched. Don't ask stupid questions!

(turns back)

I don't mind if trees move, you don't mind if trees move, it is what they are up to that will scare your panties off. A moving tree, and I have video on this, give me a little help here. *(scary music)* Coming up on a night walking human or say people having sex in a Subaru Forrester on a lonely promontory overlooking Vail, Colorado… That tree will enwrap said person or vehicle in its roots and crush that entity utterly like a python before the first light of dawn.

(points in the air)

Absorbed!

(turns on another audience member)

Don't argue with me about things that you do not understand, I told you I had video!

(back to addressing the whole)

They are learning to hunt cooperatively. Eventually whole forests will attack buildings and crush them as if they were nothing but origami swans.

(arms wide)

But do you understand why? Can you see past your antiquated 18th century views on Botany? This is not paranormal, this is science!

(attacking again)

Do not look away from me. Concentrate!

(back to the whole)

What does a tree need to live? Yes water, water, H20. What isn't there enough of? Water. If a tree senses the water table dropping, as it is internationally, as lakes and rivers dry up, where can it find a high density water source? Humans. We are 70% water, duh!

(lowering her voice)

They are coming for us. I have time lapse photography of trees leaking blood. Sir, what is your name? Well, _____ they prefer men who have recently masturbated. We're not sure why yet. So if you or any other gentleman have had their hands underneath their programs during my lecture, I suggest you leave in groups.

(back to full tone)

I quote Tolstoy, what then are we to do? When nature itself revolts, when a quiet hike is a horror story, when you cannot be safe even if the tree is deciduous, what course then must humanity take? Make no mistake it is Hobsons choice. If we destroy the trees we destroy the environment, if we leave the trees they destroy us. The answer, of course is Mars... Yes, Mars. Winds, clouds, ancient riverbeds, but no trees. My company...

(She hears something.)

Wait. There is something in the lobby.

> *(We hear it.)*

That scraping, that high-pitched scraping. The distinctive cry of the quaking Aspen, the warning growl of the Lodge pole Pine. They are coming. Quick get down between the rows. Get down! Are you crazy? Do you want to be absorbed?

> *(There are poundings and scrapings on the lobby door.)*

Too late, they've heard us.

> *(Pounding backstage.)*

My God, they're backstage. There's no place to run. Shhh.

> *(Some leaves fall from above.)*

They are coming through the roof! There's only one chance. Simulate. Pretend to be trees!

> *(Two people in the audience standup extending their arms.)*

Yes. Good. Good.

> *(A third one stands.)*

Excellent! But more like a flowering Dogwood.

> *(Person sticks a twig with flowers on it in her mouth.)*

That's it. That's it. Now bend in the wind. Bend!

> *(They do.)*

No rustle. Rustle louder. Creak.

> *(They do.)*

Yes, we have a chance. A few of us will survive. But, whatever you do, don't masturbate.

> *(blackout)*